SHHHH

KEVIN HENKES

Greenwillow Books, New York

**To Laura, with thanks and love
for this (and every) book**

Acrylic paints were used
for the full-color art.
The text type is ITC Kabel.

Printed in Hong Kong by
South China Printing Co.
First Edition
10 9 8 7 6 5 4 3 2 1

Library of Congress
Cataloging-in-Publication Data

Henkes, Kevin.
Shhhh/Kevin Henkes.
p. cm.
Summary:
A little girl quietly explores
her sleeping house before
she wakes everyone up.
ISBN 0-688-07985-7.
ISBN 0-688-07986-5 (lib. bdg.)
[1. Sleep—Fiction.
2. Family life—Fiction.]
I. Title.
PZ7.H389Si 1989
[E]—dc19
88-18771 CIP AC

SHHHH...

Everything is quiet.
Everyone is sleeping.

Lion and Bear and Bunny are quiet.
They're sleeping on my blanket.

The cat is quiet.
She's sleeping in her box.

The dog is quiet.
He's sleeping on his rug.

The baby is quiet.

She's sleeping in her crib.

Mama and Papa are quiet.

They're sleeping in their bed.

SHHHH...

Everything is quiet.
Everyone is sleeping—

GOOD MORNING, CAT!

UNTIL I WAKE

GOOD MORNING, LION AND BEAR AND BUNNY!

GOOD MORNING, DOG!

GOOD MORNING, BABY!

GOOD MORNING, MAMA!

THEM UP!

GOOD MORNING, PAPA!